P9-CRE-068

James Solheim

Grandmas ARE Greater THAN Great

PICTURES BY
Derek Desierto

GREENWILLOW BOOKS
An Imprint of HarperCollins*Publishers*

Grandmas Are Greater Than Great

For information address HarperCollins Children's Books,
a division of HarperCollins Publishers, 195 Broadway, New York, NY 10007.
www.harpercollinschildrens.com

The art is composed of collaged photographs and digitally produced line art and shape.
The text type is 22-point Archer Medium

Library of Congress Cataloging-in-Publication Data

Names: Solheim, James, author. | Desierto, Derek, illustrator.
Title: Grandmas are greater than great / by James Solheim ; pictures by Derek Desierto.
Description: First edition. | New York, NY : Greenwillow Books, an imprint of HarperCollinsPublishers, [2021] | Audience: Ages 4-8. | Audience: Grades K-1. | Summary: "Vignettes of daily life, and its delights and challenges over hundreds of years, that make us the product of each daughter, mother, and grandma who came before us"—Provided by publisher. Includes note about how math applies to generations, and a chart of four generations of grandmothers.
Identifiers: LCCN 2020035289 | ISBN 9780062671233 (hardback)
Subjects: CYAC: Great-grandmothers—Fiction. | Grandmothers—Fiction. | Mother and child—Fiction.
Classification: LCC PZ7.S689 Gr 2021 | DDC [E]—dc23
LC record available at https://lccn.loc.gov/2020035289
21 22 23 24 25 RTLO 10 9 8 7 6 5 4 3 2 1
First Edition

Greenwillow Books

For Joyce, Jenny, Justin, Jeanette,
Jerome, and grandmas worldwide
—J. S.

To my grandmothers—Epifania, Emilia, and Rosa.
All of whom were greater than great.
—D. D.

You come from grandmas of grandmas
of grandmas of grandmas of grandmas,
going back thousands of years.

You needed them all
for you to be you.

Many grandmas ago,

one

great

great

great

great

great

great

great

great

grandma held a baby day and night, hugging her back to health. And when the child was well again, they both wore big, red hollyhock flowers for hats to celebrate. And the baby let out her first laugh.

That baby grew up to be your

great

great

great

great

great

great

great

grandma.

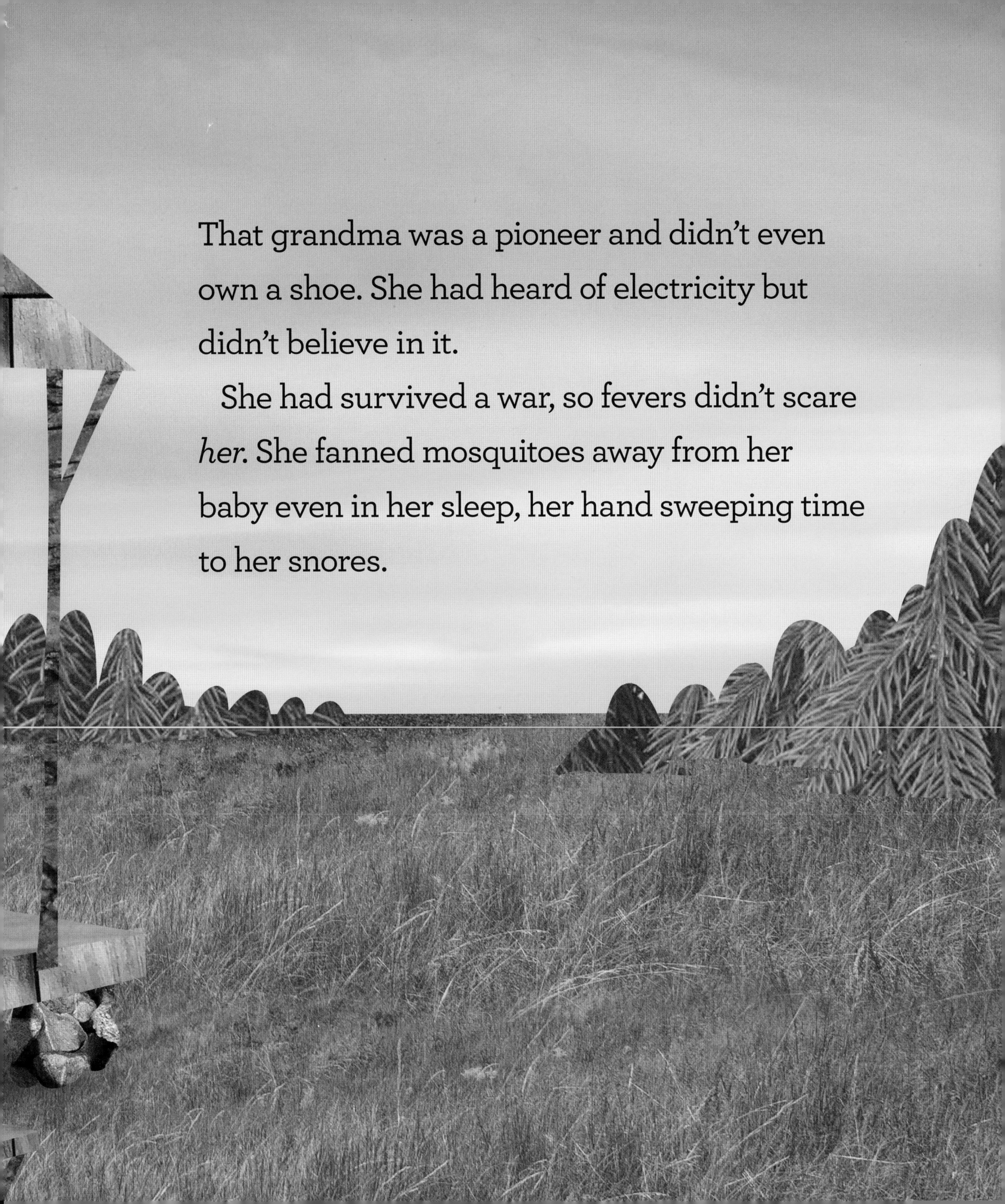

That grandma was a pioneer and didn't even own a shoe. She had heard of electricity but didn't believe in it.

She had survived a war, so fevers didn't scare *her*. She fanned mosquitoes away from her baby even in her sleep, her hand sweeping time to her snores.

That baby grew up to be your

great

great

great

great

great

great

grandma.

That grandma dreamed of her baby all grown up and fancy, in a house with real glass windows. Maybe she'd even be a teacher in her own one-room school—drawing alphabets in a sunbeam swirled with chalk dust.

ABC

Then the baby broke the family's only bowl and woke that grandma from the dream.

That baby grew up to be your

great great

great great great

grandma.

That grandma knew how to milk a goat

and fix a wagon wheel.

She knew how to rope a calf.

But she couldn't get
that misbehaving
cloth to be a diaper.
So she put her
newborn baby's
bottom in a bonnet
and showed her the stars.

That baby grew up to be your

great

great

great

great

grandma.

That grandma cuddled her baby in a sleigh
whooshing across a frozen lake.

At the lake's far end, an old woman sewed blossoms made of cloth into a quilt. Nobody could fool *her* into talking to a machine. She pulled that ringing telephone box off the wall and donated it to the chickens.

When her family arrived, she sat snoring and swatting flies in her sleep. She woke to find her new great-great-grandbaby in her arms.

That baby grew up to be your

great

great

great

grandma.

That grandma danced with her baby across the grass, laughing and laughing under the town's first streetlights. Lamps on poles really *could* light a town.

When the stars grew bright, grandma and baby rode to the cousins' house for the baby's first taste of gooseberry pie.

That baby grew up to be your

great

great

grandma.

That grandma took her kids fishing every day so all seven of them could eat. She led them through fields, digging potatoes the harvesters had overlooked. She stuffed a room from floor to ceiling with potatoes to feed her family through the winter. They needed every one.

And she still found time to have baby number eight—the exact baby you needed for you to someday be you.

That baby grew up to be your

great

grandma.

That grandma listened to the radio with her baby, and twirled with her baby among the tall trees, giving her baby baths just to keep her in a world of love and bubbles and no wars.

After hundreds of baths, she turned the radio on and hollered with joy at what she heard, hugging her baby up out of the water and running outside to find someone, anyone, who could tell her if it was true—the war was over!

That baby grew up to be your

grandma.

That grandma swung her baby high up out of the crowd. Sitting on strong, slender shoulders, the child could see everything now—from sun to storm clouds to the band's loud guitars. It was like being the world's tallest person.

When the rain came, the concert ended, but not their dancing. This was the baby's first chance ever to splash in rain and drink it straight from the sky.

That baby grew up to be your mother.

Your mother was about to meet someone for the first time. Someone who had never seen light or tasted air, someone who didn't know how to walk, talk, or even breathe. Your mother had so much to teach and share, and so many hugs built up inside her, just waiting.

Tiny hands reached out to her from a nurse's arms.

Click-click-CLICK-click, click-click-click.

Pictures flew at millions of miles an hour to far-off phones, igniting instant cheers.

Someone had arrived—

SOAP

And who are you?

You're a hollyhock hat and a grandma's snore,

a gleeful squeal scattering chalk-dust dreams,

a baby's bare bottom in a bonnet under stars,

a giggle and a gurgle blossoming from a quilt,

a gooseberry pucker in a candlelit kitchen,

a potato-stuffed room and a soapy shout of joy,

a dance in the rain and a mother's first hug.

One hug among millions
that took thousands of years
to add up to you.

Math uncovers the world's unexpected secrets. Did you know that you come from one unique mom, two grandmas, and four great-grandmas? Going back from there, the numbers in each generation keep doubling. Doubling makes numbers go up very fast. In only a few centuries, you're up to millions of grandmas who are greater than great!